Gone Forever!
Diplodocus

Rupert Matthews

Heinemann Library
Chicago, Illinois

Customer Service 888-454-2279

Visit our website at www.heinemannlibrary.com

Designed by Ron Kamen and Paul Davies & Associates
Ilustrations by Maureen and Gordon Gray, James Field (SGA), and Darren Lingard
Originated by Ambassador Litho Ltd.
Printed and bound in China by South China Printing Company

07 06 05 04 03
10 9 8 7 6 5 4 3 2 1

Library of Congress Cataloging-in-Publication Data
Matthews, Rupert.
  Diplodocus / Rupert Matthews.
    p. cm. -- (Gone forever)
Includes index.
Summary: Describes what has been learned about the size, behavior, and surroundings of the long-extinct dinosaur known as diplodocus.
  ISBN 1-40340-788-6 (HC), 1-4034-3416-6 (Pbk)
  1. Diplodocus--Juvenile literature. [1. Diplodocus. 2. Dinosaurs.] I. Title. II. Series.
  QE862.S3 T333 2003
  567.913--dc21

                    2002003698

Acknowledgments
The author and publishers are grateful to the following for permission to reproduce copyright material:
pp. 4 Ardea; pp. 6, 10, 18, 20, 24 Francois Gohier/Ardea; p. 8 Science Photo Library; pp. 12, 22, 26 Natural History Museum, London; p. 14 Mark Newman/FLPA; p. 16 Rodolfo Coria/REUTERS.
Cover photograph reproduced with permission of Francois Gohier/Ardea.

Every effort has been made to contact copyright holders of any material reproduced in this book. Any omissions will be rectified in subsequent printings if notice is given to the publisher.
Special thanks to Dr. Peter Mackovicky for his review of this book.

Some words are shown in bold, **like this.** You can find out what they mean by looking in the glossary.

Contents

Gone Forever!

Sometimes, all the animals of one kind die. This means they are **extinct.** Scientists study extinct animals by looking at **fossils.** Many animals that lived millions of years ago are extinct.

One of these extinct animals was a **dinosaur** called Diplodocus. This huge animal lived about 150 million years ago. Most of the other animals and plants that lived then are also now extinct.

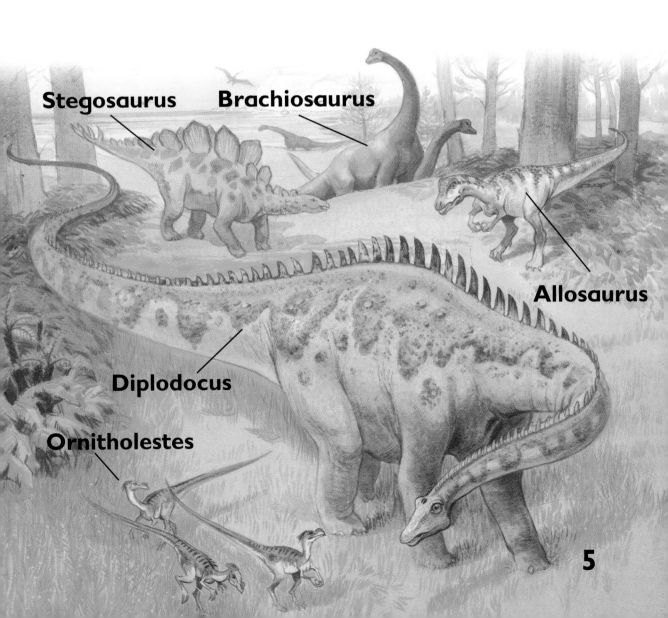

Stegosaurus

Brachiosaurus

Allosaurus

Diplodocus

Ornitholestes

Diplodocus' Home

Some scientists study rocks. They use the rocks to find out what an area was like when the rocks were formed. They can even tell what the weather was like.

Scientists know that Diplodocus lived in areas where it rained a lot for some of the year. At other times it was dry. The land was flat with wide rivers, lakes, and swamps. There were some open spaces, but also many trees and other plants.

Plants

Sometimes, plants are turned into **fossils.**
These fossils tell us which plants were alive
when the rocks were formed.

fossils of ginkgo leaves

There were no grasses or flowers when Diplodocus
lived. Instead **ferns, fir trees,** and **cycads** like
those that grow today were common. Other plants
that lived then are **extinct.**

9

Living with Diplodocus

Fossils show that many other animals lived at the same time as Diplodocus. Some of these animals were also large **dinosaurs,** such as **Stegosaurus.** Fossils of smaller animals, such as **mammals,** frogs, and small **reptiles,** have also been found.

Stegosaurus fossil

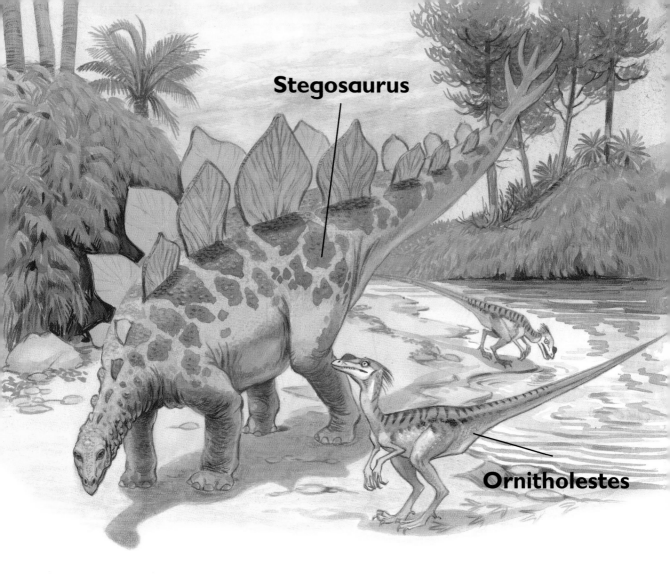

Stegosaurus

Ornitholestes

Stegosaurus was a plant-eating dinosaur. It was almost as long as a school bus and weighed almost four and a half tons. It used spikes on its tail to fight enemies. Smaller dinosaurs included **Ornitholestes.** Ornitholestes hunted lizards and other small animals.

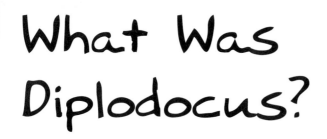

What Was Diplodocus?

Several **fossils** of Diplodocus have been found. The bones were dug out of the ground and put together. The bones show what Diplodocus looked like.

Diplodocus had a very long neck and an even longer tail. It was about the length of three school buses put together! It walked on four very strong legs. Diplodocus ate only plants.

Diplodocus Eggs

dinosaur egg fossils

Scientists have found **fossils** of eggs laid by other **dinosaurs** like Diplodocus. The eggs are about the size of soccer balls.

No one has found any Diplodocus nests, so we do not know much about them. Perhaps a mother Diplodocus dug a hole in soft ground with her feet. The hole would have been shallow, or not too deep. Then, she put her eggs in the hole.

Growing Up

Fossils of baby **dinosaurs** show that they were much, much smaller than adults. But they grew quickly. A baby Diplodocus probably doubled in weight every month.

fossil of a baby dinosaur like Diplodocus

16

Diplodocus babies probably lived in thick forests. There, they could hide among the plants and be safe from large hunting dinosaurs. They probably stayed in the forests for about five years, while they grew bigger and stronger.

A Herd on the Move

Fossils of footprints made by **dinosaurs** like Diplodocus have been found in rocks. These footprints show that Diplodocus probably lived in small **herds.** Only footprints of adult or half-grown animals have been found in herds.

Some scientists think that the half-grown animals stayed in the center of each herd. The larger animals could then protect them. Other scientists think the younger animals followed the adults.

Reaching for Food

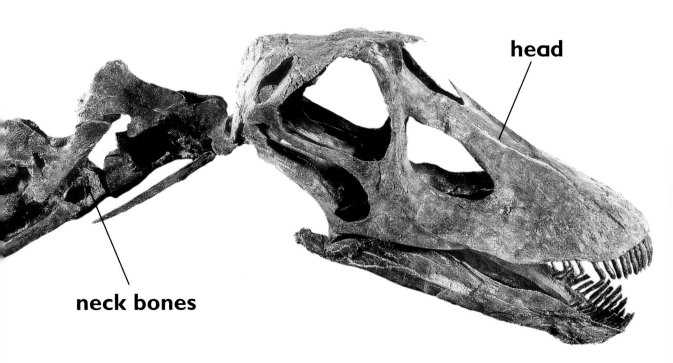

head

neck bones

Diplodocus had a very long neck. **Fossil** bones show that its neck and head were usually held straight out in front of the body. The long tail helped to balance its heavy neck.

Diplodocus could bend its neck from side to side or up and down. It could reach many different plants while standing still. Diplodocus would eat all the plants it could reach, and then move on.

Unusual Teeth

The head of Diplodocus was small for its body. Its jaw muscles were quite weak. Its teeth were long and straight like the teeth of a comb. This meant Diplodocus could not chew its food.

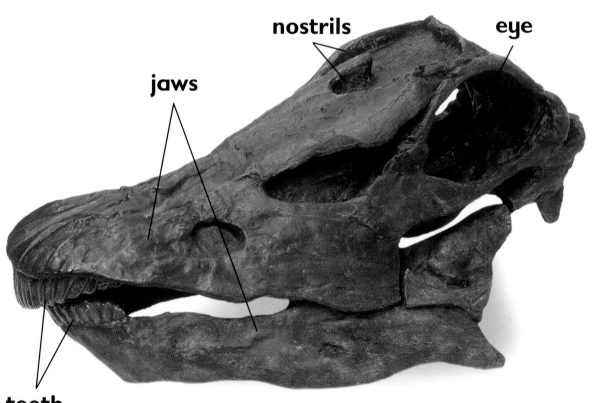

nostrils

eye

jaws

teeth

Scientists believe that Diplodocus had a special way of eating. It closed its mouth around a tree branch, and then pulled back. The teeth dragged the leaves off the tree like a rake, leaving the branches behind. Then Diplodocus swallowed the leaves whole.

Danger!

Scientists have found **fossils** of **dinosaurs** with two legs and long, sharp teeth. **Allosaurus** was one of these dinosaurs. It killed and ate other dinosaurs. Allosaurus lived at the same time as Diplodocus.

Allosaurus skeleton

Allosaurus was about half as long as Diplodocus and was very strong. It used its claws and teeth to attack other dinosaurs. Allosaurus probably attacked young Diplodocus. They would have been easier to kill than the large adults.

Fighting Diplodocus

Diplodocus had a long tail with strong muscles. It could swish its tail from side to side very quickly. Diplodocus could use the end of its tail like a powerful whip.

Scientists think that Diplodocus may have used its tail to fight. For example, **Allosaurus** would attack using its teeth and claws. If Diplodocus hit Allosaurus with its tail, Allosaurus could be badly hurt. Diplodocus could then escape.

Where Did Diplodocus Live?

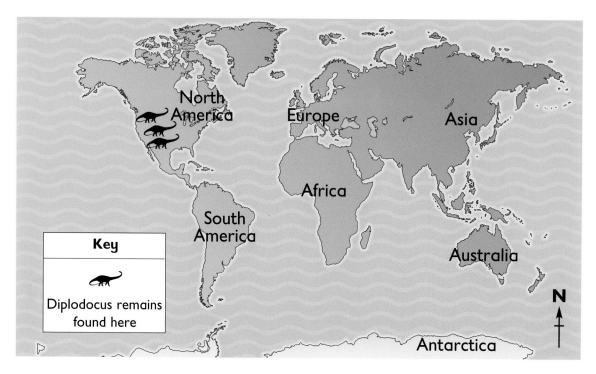

Key

Diplodocus remains found here

North America

Europe

Asia

Africa

South America

Australia

Antarctica

N

Diplodocus **fossils** have been found in North America. These show that it lived in the western part of North America. Other **dinosaurs** that looked like Diplodocus have been found in Asia, Europe, and parts of Africa.

When Did Diplodocus Live?

Diplodocus lived between 155 and 144 million years ago. This was the time that scientists call the Jurrasic Period. It was during the time known as the Age of Dinosaurs.

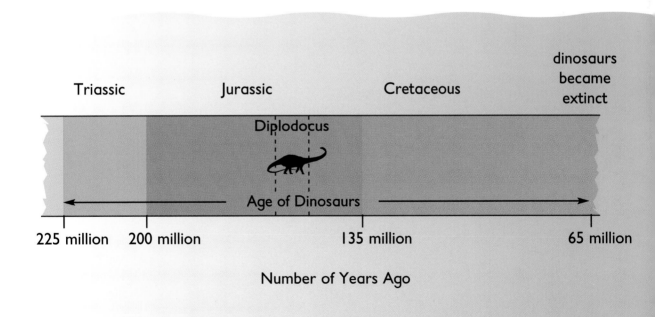

Number of Years Ago

Fact File

Diplodocus	
Length:	up to 89 feet (27 meters)
Height:	up to 20 feet (6 meters)
Weight:	22 tons (20 metric tons)
Time:	Late Jurassic Period, about 150 million years ago
Place:	North America

How to Say It

Allosaurus—al-ah-sor-us
cycad—si-cad
dinosaur—dine-ah-sor

Diplodocus—dip-lah-dah-kus
Stegosaurus—steg-ah-sor-us

Glossary

Allosaurus large meat-eating dinosaur that hunted Diplodocus, Stegosaurus, and other plant-eating dinosaurs

cycad type of plant that looks like a short palm tree

dinosaur one of a large group of extinct reptiles that lived on Earth millions of years ago

extinct no longer living on Earth

fern plant with long leaves that grows in wet places

fir tree tree that keeps its leaves all year. The leaves are skinny and stay green.

fossil remains of a plant or animal, usually found in rocks. Most fossils are from hard parts like bones and teeth. Some fossils are traces of animals, such as their footprints.

herd group of animals that lives together

mammal animal with hair or fur. Mammals give birth to live young instead of laying eggs.

Ornitholestes type of dinosaur that lived at the same time as Diplodocus. It ate lizards and other small animals.

reptile cold-blooded animals such as a modern snake or lizard

Stegosaurus type of plant-eating dinosaur that lived at the same time as Diplodocus

More Books to Read

Cohen, Daniel. *Diplodocus*. Mankato, Minn.: Capstone Press, 2003.

Goecke, Michael P. *Diplodocus*. Edina, Minn.: Abdo Publishing Company, 2002.

Olshevsky, George. *Diplodocus*. Mankato, Minn.: Smart Apple Media, 2002.

Index